Make Room
for RAGS

LAURA BANNON

Make Room for RAGS

Illustrated by Vee Guthrie

HOUGHTON MIFFLIN COMPANY BOSTON

The author is grateful to Mr. and Mrs. Gilbert Loudon who told her intriguing stories about their farm animals.

She is also indebted to Mr. and Mrs. F. C. Smith of Blanco, Texas and their charming family who form the background for MAKE ROOM FOR RAGS. They included the author as a member of the household while she gathered information for the story.

PUBLISHED BY HOUGHTON MIFFLIN COMPANY, DISTRIBUTED TO THE SCHOOLS BY XEROX EDUCATION PUBLICATIONS

LIBRARY OF CONGRESS CATALOG CARD NUMBER 64-19381
ISBN: 0-395-15496-0 REINFORCED EDITION
PRINTED IN THE U.S.A.

CONTENTS

BAD DOG, RAGS

Danny was getting ready to help Dad feed the goats. He sat on the front steps of the farmhouse and jammed his right foot into a muddy boot. He was about to pull on the other boot when he stopped to listen.

"Drop it," he shouted.

He knew that sound—that low teasing growl and the weak mewing. He hop-skipped through the wet grass to the backyard.

"Drop it, I say."

The half-grown dog dropped the kitten she was shaking. It scooted up the oak

tree to join the rest of the cat family
that had been chased there. They sat in
a row, watching the dog with their sea-
green eyes.

"Bad dog, Rags," Danny scolded. He
reached for his dog's collar but Rags
ducked and dashed away, inviting Danny
to chase her. She scattered the squawking
chickens and slid under the barnyard fence
where the mules were penned.

Molly, the meanest of the mules, snorted
and reared up, ready to strike with her
sharp hoofs.

Rags darted back like a shot, straight
into the protection of Danny's arms.

"You just have to learn some manners,"
Danny told her. His voice was tough but
his fingers were kind as they ran through

her shaggy fur. "I guess you had a bad start for a dog."

Danny was thinking of the night Rags came out of nowhere. She came whimpering to the farmhouse door, shivering from the sleet that pelted the Texas hill country.

Of course Rags had to be taken in. But Danny was the only one in the whole family who thought they should make room for Rags to stay.

He remembered that Mom said, "We are already overrun with animals. We have to save a little room on this farm for people."

But she rubbed Rags dry with a towel and fed her.

And Danny remembered that Dad said that pup would never be worth a hoot at herding stock.

Danny pulled on his other boot and said aloud to Rags, "I knew right away you were as smart as a whip. And I promised Dad I would train you. But you won't be serious long enough to give me a chance. And you shouldn't run off, all over the neighborhood. The first time a pack of dogs gets into trouble you will be blamed along with the others."

Rags gave Danny a quick slathering kiss on the cheek with her wet tongue. She plainly thought he was tops. And did that count!

"I should tie you up, you rascal," Danny said. "But come along to the pasture. Maybe I can teach you to have some manners with the goats."

DAISY AND HER KID

Dad came out of the barn and loaded a sack of grain into the jeep. Danny's younger sister, Holly, had already climbed into the front seat.

"I'm going too," she announced. "I want to see if there are any new baby goats."

A little thing like a biting March wind couldn't keep Holly from going to the pasture at kidding time.

Danny helped Dad finish loading the grain. Then he jumped into the back of the jeep and stood, bouncing, while Dad drove down the steep pasture road.

Suddenly, with a jolt and screech of brakes, he stopped the jeep.

"That fool dog!" he exploded. "Stopping to scratch fleas in front of a moving jeep! Something has to be done about her."

Danny jumped down and boosted Rags into the jeep. He held her in his lap while they rattled up the next hill toward the pasture gate.

The goats were already streaming over
the hills to the feed troughs near the
gate. The nannies were bleating and the
kids were answering in their thin piping
voices.

The clatter of the jeep brought the flock on the run better than any goat call. That sound meant food — food they needed so as to make up for the lack of grass this cold spring.

When Rags began to bark at the goats they stopped in their tracks. Heads jerked up, ears pointed forward.

"Keep that dog quiet," Dad said. "She gets the goats all stirred up."

Danny held Rags's mouth shut until they reached the gate. Then he handed Rags to Holly and said, "Don't let her bark." He let down the bars to the gate and closed them again after the jeep passed through. And he helped Dad scatter grain in the long feed troughs.

Holly stood watching the last of the

flock racing to the troughs. "Daisy has her
baby," she squealed.

She quickly handed Rags to Danny. Then
she ran to the spotted nanny that trailed
behind the flock. Daisy was nuzzling a
tiny kid that tagged along on wobbly
legs.

Dad examined Daisy and her kid. "You came through fine, old girl," he said. "But I was sure you would at least give us twins."

He decided they had better look the pasture over to see if there were any newborn kids in need of help.

Danny knew what Dad had in mind. A nanny can be as affectionate as any dog. But sometimes she doesn't make a good mother. She may go off to find food for herself before a new baby gets its first meal. And that first meal is mighty important to a kid born out in the cold.

And sometimes if a nanny has triplets or quads she won't own them all.

RAGS MAKES A DISCOVERY

They climbed back into the jeep. Danny clutched Rags until they were well away from the goats. Then he let the pup jump out and race alongside.

First she chased a road runner that was far too swift for her to catch. At a hole in the ground she set up a racket. That was probably the door to an armadillo's home, Danny decided.

Farther over the hill Rags began barking in excited yips. She wouldn't leave the spot to follow the jeep.

Dad stopped the jeep and Danny ran to see what was up. Rags was standing over two small kids huddled in the bushes. It

was easy to tell from the creamy white of
their fur that they were very young.

"Rags has found two little goats," Danny
shouted. "She hasn't touched them. She
was just letting us know they were there."

His voice soared. And why not? This was
the first time his dog had shown any sense.

Danny carried the kids to the jeep. Dad said he was pretty sure they belonged to Daisy because of their black spots. "We'll take them to her," he said. "Maybe we can get her to feed them."

But Daisy had her own ideas about that. She sniffed them but wouldn't let them nurse. Off she walked, talking softly to her favorite triplet who tagged along.

Holly cuddled the two little outcasts. "We have to take them to the house and bring them up ourself, don't we Daddy?" She sounded glad.

"Seems that's the best we can do," Dad told her.

FINDERS KEEPERS

When Holly and Danny carried the kids
into the house, the family gathered around
to admire them.

Judy, the older sister, examined the
small hoofs and delicate deerlike faces.
"They are made so carefully," she said.

And then she hunted for Coke bottles and
the long nipples to fit on the bottles.

Mom laughed a little and said, "We'll
make pets of them. And they'll expect to
move into the house every time we open the
door. Which of you children will be willing
to move out to make room for them?"

"Not I," said five-year-old Nelson who
was holding one of the kids. "I won't move

out but I'll move over and let them sleep
with me."

Mom poured milk in a pan to warm for
the kids. She thinned it with a dash of

water and sweetened it with a bit of sugar.

Danny went to the barn and put a thick layer of straw into a grocery box. He noticed that Rags didn't follow him as she usually did. She stayed close to the kids and sniffed them with an eager look on her funny face.

Everyone watched while the kids were fed and bedded in the box which was placed behind the stove. Rags lay down beside the box.

"This is something new for Rags," Danny said. "Instead of teasing the goats she is watching over them. Probably she thinks finders keepers."

After many feedings and a day and a night in the box, the kids decided to journey out into the world. The first to wobble out of the box was the one with a black nose. His legs were shaky but he had a strong bunt for every flat surface he came to. So Judy gave him the name Bunter.

And because the other kid tagged along wherever her brother went, Holly decided she should be called Tagalong.

BACKYARD SOCIETY

The next day the cold north wind blew itself out and the farm was warmed by sunshine. The chickens were full of soft contented talk as they gave themselves dust baths.

Mom said, "It is time for the kids to change their address. Instead of *Kitchen of Hillside Farm* it should be *Under Backsteps.*"

Rags watched anxiously while Danny moved the box and the kids to the new address.

The kids promptly left the box to join the society of the backyard. At once they found out how much fun it is to be kids.

They had fits
of fun. They
stood on their
hind legs then
danced on all
fours.

"Look at Rags," Danny said. "She is so
busy watching the kids she's even forgotten
to chase the cats up the tree."

The ducks jabbered at their silly new
neighbors. Then they lined themselves up
and marched off to the pond for a swim.

But Lily, the leghorn hen, hopped into
the kids' box, singing softly to herself.
Soon she was telling everyone that she
had just done a pretty wonderful thing.
"Cut-cut-cut ayapayapayap," she shrilled.

Holly claimed she was trying to say, "I

just laid an egg. Hurrah! Hurrah! Hurrah!"

But Danny decided she was saying, "I lay each day yet go barefoot."

The kids were the first to see another family moving from under the house into the backyard. The little goats stood on dainty tiptoes with ears pointed forward.

They stared at what they were seeing for the first time — babies as young as themselves.

"Widdy Biddy has hatched her chicks," Holly cried and began to count them.

With coaxing clucks the pet hen kept the cheeping chicks close to her as she moved into the sunshine.

While she was gathering them under her fluffed-out wings Bunter moved in to say "Howdy." His baby face showed surprise

when he got a sharp peck on the nose.

Danny laughed and said, "Bunter doesn't know if that was a peck or a kiss."

Then the kids found Waddles, the goose, sitting on a nest in the currant bushes. She scolded them with hisses and a nip from her sharp beak. She had been sitting on an old golf ball for days. After all her loving care she wasn't going to let those two little upstarts keep her from turning the ball into a fluffy gosling.

All the while Rags followed the kids, her floppy ears alert. Holly and Danny agreed that overnight she had stopped being a silly pup and had turned into a sensible dog.

THE MEAN MULE

By now the mules were telling everyone
they wanted to be turned into the pasture.
Dad came out of the barn to open the
pasture gate. When he came back through
the barnyard he was carrying a dead
chick.

"It looks as if a mule stomped on it,"
he told Danny and Holly.

"Do you think a mule did it on purpose?" Holly asked.

Dad sat down on the steps and explained. "It's a strange thing about mules. There is often one who hates young things. I've known a number of mules that would kill any young thing on sight. Maybe it is because they can't have sons and daughters of their own."

Danny didn't have to ask why. He knew they couldn't have young because they were hybrids. One parent was a horse and the other was a donkey.

"Don't let the kids squeeze under the fence into the barnyard when the mules are there," Dad warned.

"Rags will help me keep them out," said Danny.

They all laughed at the sight under the steps. The kids were now cuddled into Rags's long fur. She was going over them lovingly with her big dog's tongue. They lifted their small faces for her caress.

Dad said as he left, "That pup is turning into a regular nanny." He had to fix the latch on the barnyard gate, he said. "Molly has been nuzzling it and she came close to opening it."

THE BABY-SITTER

The screen door slammed as Nelson elbowed his way onto the back steps. He carried a bottle of milk in each hand.

"Mom says it is time to feed Bunter and Tagalong," he announced.

Rags nosed close to the kids while they drank with sneezly, snuffly sounds and smacking lips.

"Want to help?" Danny asked Rags. He tied a handkerchief around one of the bottles and got Rags to hold the tag ends in her mouth. She rolled her eyes to watch the kids drink.

"She's catching on," Holly said, giggling. "Come see, Mom," she called.

Both Judy and Mom poked their heads out
the door and Mom said, "I would have to
see this to believe it. The pup is really

growing up. She is taking herself seriously."

After that Rags was usually on hand to hold a bottle when the kids were fed. She watched over them as carefully as Widdy Biddy cared for her chicks.

But Rags's job was much more worrisome. The kids were into everything. If they were in danger Rags barked a sharp warning.

When they climbed up the bracing pole on the barnyard gate, Rags barked so fiercely it brought Danny running. But it was a lunge and a snort from Molly that sent the kids in a flying leap to the safe side of the gate.

If the kids were in mischief that did them no harm, Rags just watched them like a doting mother with two spoiled children.

One morning Rags
watched the kids
jump from the
fence to the top
of the mailbox
where they pulled
out the morning
newspaper and
scattered it to
the winds.

Each day the kids learned to climb
higher and find new ways to get into
mischief and have kid fun. But they were
so affectionate and so filled with joy
it was easy to forgive them.

When Judy came out on the porch with
a pan of vegetables to peel, she found the

kids lying in the porch swing. They had
the smug look of owning it.

"Move over," Judy said.

They didn't mind doing that. In fact
they welcomed her. When she slapped them
away from the vegetables, Tagalong chewed
the buttons on her dress. And Bunter
nibbled at her back hair and talked softly
into her ear.

In the end Judy swung them to sleep.

AUNT MINNIE

After breakfast one morning Mom said
to Judy and Holly, "Now see that your room
is made up neatly. Your Aunt Minnie is
driving through from Austin and is stopping
by for lunch. You know how prim she is.
She sees the dust before she sees the
furniture."

Everyone got busy—even Nelson who
had been putting together a jigsaw puzzle.
He left it to water the house plants and
fill the drinking trough in the backyard.

When a sparkling new car purred up the
drive and Danny saw the wave of a white
glove, he shouted, "Aunt Minnie is here."

The family poured out the front door

to greet her. And Nelson charged through the house to join them. Aunt Minnie always remembered how well he could put together jigsaw puzzles. Each time she came she brought him a bigger one that was harder to solve.

Aunt Minnie was given a noisy welcome while she emptied her car of presents she had brought to each of the family.

She stopped to look at a bed of geraniums while Mom explained that they were doing all right until the orphan goats began to nip off the flowers as soon as they budded.

When they all entered the house there was dead silence for a few awful seconds. The backdoor was wide open as Nelson had left it.

Tagalong was on the table finishing
the bowl of salad Mom had made for lunch.
Bunter had moved over to the sofa and was
gleefully scattering stuffings from a
cushion. When his beloved family came
through the door he was caught up in a
flurry of joy. He flung himself into the
air and landed on bouncing feet.

Mom's laugh sounded half like crying. "Those kids will simply have to be put to pasture. If they can eat my green salad they can eat pasture grass."

"But Mom," Danny said, "they're not yet three months old. They still need milk."

When he shooed the goats out of the house they leaped from the doorway. They were too filled with fun and too crowded for fun time to use the steps.

Rags calmly followed the goats and Mom said, "Look at that dog. Why didn't she warn us? I do believe she encourages the kids in their pranks.

"You don't understand Rags," Danny said. "She didn't see anything wrong in what the kids were doing. She raises a fuss only when they are in danger."

Aunt Minnie took off her gloves and sat down in a straight-backed chair. "My stars!" she exclaimed. "It seems to me it is the family that's in danger. I declare I don't know how you put up with all the confusion, Jean—" That was Mom's name.

Nelson decided to set things straight by explaining matters to Aunt Minnie. "You see," he said, "the goats feel at home inside the house because at first they lived in here with us. Bunter and Tagalong haven't found out yet they are goats. They think they are people like us."

Mom began making another salad, chatting gaily the while, but it was uphill work.

Dad came into the house and excused himself for not being on hand when Aunt Minnie arrived. "I've been mending the pasture fence where our cows broke through into Saddler's cornfield," he said.

While they ate lunch, Dad and Aunt Minnie talked a lot about the relatives because she and Dad were brother and sister.

When the time came for her to leave, Mom said in a low voice to Danny, "See that the goats are out of sight."

Danny understood how Mom felt. It was just as well for Aunt Minnie to be on her way without seeing two smart-aleck kids overrunning the porch swing.

But they weren't on the porch. They were calmly viewing their friendly world from the top of Aunt Minnie's new car. There they lounged and enjoyed a second chewing of Mom's green salad.

Rags, who didn't care for mountain climbing, lay in the shade, watching them.

"Get off, you rascals." Danny kept his voice low but made up for it by waving his arms.

The kids loved any kind of attention. They rose to their feet, looked down at Danny's wild motions, and decided it was a game. They began to prance and slide on the well-waxed surface.

Aunt Minnie came out on the porch in time to catch the goat act at its best. She sank into the porch swing and wailed "I had the car put in perfect condition."

Dad did what he could to rub off the smudges and scratches from Aunt Minnie's car. And after it disappeared down the River Road he had his say.

NO ROOM FOR RAGS

"This settles the matter," said Dad. "The goats must go to pasture. We can take bottles to them along with the feed. One bottle a day will have to do."

Danny held his breath, afraid of what Dad would say next.

"And we'll have to find another home for your dog, Danny. We don't have room on this farm for useless animals."

"Can't we wait for just one more week until we find a really good home for Rags?" Danny begged. "I'll find a way to keep the kids out of mischief."

Mom said, "I think we can wait."

But Dad didn't answer Danny. He left to

inspect the cattle and the pasture fences.

That afternoon Holly, Nelson, and Danny rolled a barrel into the backyard and nailed a springboard to it. At once the kids knew what use to make of it. They crowded each other for turns to leap from the board.

The children doubled over laughing at their fancy twists and turns.

The chickens scattered to quieter grounds and the cats ran up the oak tree.

Mom called from the kitchen, "Children, will you see if old Rhody has hidden her nest in the haymow? She has been cackling from that direction."

Danny held Rags's head between his two hands and spoke earnestly to her. "You keep the goats here. Understand?"

Rags's tail thumped agreement to whatever Danny might be saying.

Holly, Nelson, and Danny searched the haymow for Rhody's nest. But their search was cut short by the sounds that came from the backyard.

The ducks were quacking, the chickens were squawking, and Rags was barking excitedly. When Danny heard a mule snort

and then a dull thud, his stomach and
heart changed places.

The children slid from the mow and raced
through the open gate of the barnyard.

RAGS THE FIGHTER

The mules were out of their pen and loose in the backyard. They stood around the two kids. Molly was rearing up on her hind legs and striking at them with her front hoofs.

The kids were dodging the strikes with quick leaps. "H-e-e-elp! H-e-elp!" they were calling in piping bleats.

Each time Molly's front feet hit the sod she struck out with her hind legs to kick Rags who was nipping at her heels. The dog's teeth were bared and an awful growl rumbled in her throat.

Brave little Rags who had always been afraid of Molly was now fighting her

fiercely. After each nip Rags squatted so
Molly kicked over her head.

Danny grabbed a stick and started after the mules. Then he heard Dad call, "I'll stop them, son." He was returning from the pasture, leading the gentle old cow Buttercup. He dropped the rope and raced across the yard, shouting.

But before he reached the mules, a blow from Molly's heel hit Rags and sent her flying. She sprawled, limp on the grass. Danny ran to her and picked her up.

Dad had no trouble driving the mules back into the barnyard. They were afraid of him. "That blame Molly is too smart for her own good," he scolded. "She un-latched the gate."

Then Dad examined Rags and said, "I think she is just stunned—got the day-lights knocked out of her. She's a plucky pup, all right."

"She probably
saved Tagalong's
and Bunter's lives,"
said Danny. And
he told himself
that surely now
they would always
make room for Rags
on the farm.

Danny carried his dog into the house.
The family could find no wounds on her.
But they wrapped her in a blanket and
made a place for her in the kitchen. She
opened her eyes and said "Thank you" by
a faint wag of her tail.

"She's enjoying the attention," Mom
said. "Whether or not she is hurt she
must be very tired. She has earned the
right to play sick for a while."

Rags fell asleep with a healthy snore
and Holly and Danny went to find the
goats.

THE KIDS GO TO PASTURE

The backyard was quiet. The ducks and geese had gone off to the pond. The cat family had climbed out of the tree to sun themselves. Buttercup now lay in the shade where Dad had tied her.

And where were Bunter and Tagalong? They had settled themselves on Buttercup's soft-cushioned back. Sleepy-eyed, they chewed their cuds in comfort. And Buttercup seemed not to mind at all.

When Dad loaded the kids into the jeep they were, at first, only curious. But when Holly and Danny climbed in with them they were delighted. They were being taken for a ride as members of the family. Bunter breathed down Danny's neck and picked off his cap. Tagalong wiped her mouth on Holly's shoulder, then nuzzled her ear.

But when the kids were left in the pasture you never heard such wailing. They called after the jeep in voices that asked "Why?" Then their bleats changed to "Don't do this to us."

As the jeep sped over the hill, Danny and Holly heard the kids' bossy bleats telling them, "We want to go home too." "We'll play with them in the morning when we take milk to them," Danny and Holly told each other.

RAGS A SHEEP KILLER?

By the time Holly and Danny reached home, Rags had decided she had been sick long enough. She spent some time searching for the kids and then she disappeared.

Danny called and called but no Rags. Was she still hunting for the kids or had she joined her dog friends in the neighborhood? Danny hoped she hadn't.

Rags didn't return for supper and when Danny went to bed, still no Rags.

Very early the next morning, while the family was having breakfast, Mr. Saddler called at the house.

"I wonder where your dog was last night," he said. "A pack of dogs killed two of my sheep."

Dad said the thing that was expected of him. "If our dog had any part of this, of course we'll get rid of her. But I'd first like to make sure she was with the pack. Has anyone seen her since yesterday?" Dad asked the family.

No. No one had seen Rags since late afternoon.

Killing sheep was a serious thing. Danny felt as if he had fallen down a well.

Mr. Saddler left to call on other neighbors who owned dogs.

Soon after he left, the family heard a scratch on the door. Danny ran to open it and found Rags, soaking wet. Beside her stood a bedraggled Bunter.

"Rags has brought Bunter back from the

pasture," Danny shouted. "She hasn't been killing sheep. She has been with the kids all night."

But where was Tagalong? Rags was trying to tell them about that. She plainly wanted Danny to follow her.

Dad said, "We'll drive down to the goat pasture and see what's up."

Bunter was left to be taken care of by Mom who said, "I give up."

Rags rode to the pasture in the back of the jeep with Holly and Danny. She seemed to be contented with the direction they were going. But when they came near the pasture she jumped out of the jeep and led them to the place where a brook ran under the fence.

They heard Tagalong before they saw her. Her tired bleat told the world, "This is a-a-awful ba-a-ad, b-a-a-ad!"

And then they saw her — up to her neck in water. She had slid into a chuckhole and couldn't climb up the slippery bank. Tracks showed where Rags had led the goats

out of the pasture through the gap caused
by the brook.

On the way home everyone was happy.
Rags smoothed Tagalong's matted coat. And
Tagalong showed her relief by kissing
everyone she could reach with her quick
tongue.

Dad was in a good mood too. "We are probably the only family in Texas who has a full-time baby-sitter for orphaned goats," he said. "But we'll have to teach the sitter to give up the babies when it is time for them to be put to pasture."

"I'll keep Rags tied up until they join the flock," Danny said.

A NEW JOB FOR RAGS

When Danny woke the next morning he looked out the window and saw a funny sight. Bunter had his head pressed against Rags's head and was playfully pushing her backward across the yard. She was no match for the half-grown goat.

And now the goats were big enough to have big ideas. After teasing Rags, Bunter stood straight up on his hind legs and began to pull clothes off the clothesline.

Danny ran out and stopped Bunter. Then he coaxed Rags into the house and kept her there while Holly and Dad took the kids to pasture.

When the jeep returned, Danny called out,

"Did the kids make a fuss about being left
in the pasture?"

"They didn't mind too much," Holly told
him. "Maybe they expect Rags to come for
them. But wait till you see what I have."

She was carrying a day-old, black,
orphaned goat. They fed it and made a bed
for it. And Rags lay down beside the box
to watch over her new charge.

Mom laughed and said, "Here we go again."